Animal Tails

Friends of Faith™

A Division of Faith Books & MORE
Suwanee, GA

AUTHORS

Pat Orrell ◆ Corinne Koonz Pushman ◆ Erin Vannoy ◆ Emily Vannoy ◆ Vicki Westling

ILLUSTRATORS

Annette Asbill ◆ Jim O'Connell ◆ Matthew Smiley ◆ Emily Vannoy

First published by Faith Books & MORE

ISBN: 978-0-9845779-0-3

Printed in the United States of America

A Division of Faith Books & MORE

3255 Lawrenceville-Suwanee Rd.
Suite P250
Suwanee, GA 30024
publishing@faithbooksandmore.com
www.faithbooksandmore.com

TABLE OF CONTENTS

Marjorie Elisabeth Mousie
Pat Orrell
Illustrated by: Matthew Smiley

Marjorie Elisabeth Mousie

Pat Orrell

Let me tell you the surprising story of Marjorie Elisabeth Mousie, a pretty little field mouse who was born many years ago in Holland.

How a mouse with prettier brown eyes, fluffier gray fur or more nicely shaped mouse ears would be hard to find. But dear reader, Marjorie Elisabeth Mousie was born with gigantic feet! Yes! Really big, huge, humongous feet!

Mother Mousie took out the family album and looked at pictures of Grandpa and Grandma Mousie and Great Grandpa and Great Grandma Mousie. They looked at pictures of aunts, uncles, cousins, but nowhere in the family of today or long ago could they find another mousie with such great big feet.

As you may know, Holland is very cold in the winter, and Marjorie Elisabeth Mousie's feet caused Mother Mousie a lot of trouble and worry. No matter how hard Mother Mousie tried to keep Marjorie Elisabeth Mousie wrapped in a baby blanket, her feet would always peek out.

When Marjorie Elisabeth Mousie was placed in the cradle,

her feet poked out through the end spokes and when Mother Mousie used all of her yarn to knit big booties for Marjorie Elisabeth, one toe after another popped out the end. Mother Mousie broke down and cried!

But Marjorie Elisabeth was indeed such a sweet and good baby that everyone in the family forgot about her big feet. She grew up to be a pretty, lively mouse and life was good for Marjorie Elisabeth Mousie until the day she was old enough to go out and play.

First, it was necessary for Marjorie Elisabeth to have weekend shoes made for her like all the other Dutch children wore.

When Marjorie Elisabeth put on her new wooden shoes, they were so heavy she could not lift her feet.

So Grandpa made special shoes for Marjorie Elisabeth. The shoes had bottom soles of wood with cloth straps that went over the top of Marjorie Elisabeth's feet to hold the shoes on. Oh, how ugly and different poor Marjorie Elisabeth felt.

The children laughed and made awful fun of Marjorie Elisabeth's big feet. And even when some of the kinder children let her play with them, her feet caused all kinds of problems.

Marjorie Elisabeth couldn't play hopscotch because her feet covered two squares at once. She could not play ring-around-the-rosy because everyone in the circle tripped over her feet.

"Oh, go away, Marjorie Elisabeth," cried the children. "You are ruining all our games." So Marjorie Elisabeth had to play by herself.

Marjorie Elisabeth Mousie was so lonely! She really wanted to play with children her own age.

She was very smart at school work and the teacher praised her so but none of that made up for the loneliness Marjorie Elisabeth Mousie felt.

Sometimes when Marjorie Elisabeth Mousie was very sad she would visit Grandpa and Grandma Henrik Mouse that lived in an old windmill on the bank of a pond.

Grandpa carved lovely wooden clocks and toys. He made a beautiful mouse baby doll for Marjorie Elisabeth Mousie.

The visit to her Grandparents was one bright spot in Marjorie Elisabeth's life.

Grandma would sit with Marjorie Elisabeth Mousie in a chair by the fireplace and bring her cups of rich chocolate Dutch cocoa and Grandpa would tell Marjorie Elisabeth Mousie stories of famous mice of long ago. Soon Marjorie Elisabeth Mousie would forget all her troubles and feel very cozy and loved.

One day Mother Matilda Mouse took Marjorie Elisabeth Mousie's good pink dress from the closet and placed a lovely pink hair ribbon on Marjorie Elisabeth's dresser.

"This is a school day, Mama. Why am I going to wear my best dress?" asked Marjorie. "Because, Marjorie Elisabeth, after school today all the boys and girls in Miss Elder's fourth grade are going to dancing school!"

Oh, how wonderful, thought Marjorie Elisabeth Mousie. "I love to dance." Whenever the street organ came through the village, Marjorie Elisabeth

Mousie was the first mouse in line to pay for a favorite tune.

Marjorie Elisabeth Mousie kept her pretty pink dress very neat and clean all day and was very careful not to spill anything during lunchtime.

At the end of the day, Mrs. Elder appeared at the end of the hall. "Line up, children. Quickly now! Boys on one side, girls on the other. When I give the signal, walk to the center. Boys, bow like this." Miss Elder bowed. "And girls, curtsy like this." Miss Elder curtsied. "Then join hands like this and step together. 1-2-3, 1-2-3, glide-glide, and soon enough you will be dancing. It is really easy and fun. Now, children, begin."

The children walked to the center of the room. Bow and curtsy. But when Marjorie Elisabeth Mousie's partner tried to take her arm for dancing, he couldn't. Her feet were in the way!

"Miss Elder," yelled the boy, "how can I dance with Miss Super foot? I can't even get near her." The class began to giggle and laugh. Poor Marjorie Elisabeth Mousie. She ran out.

This time she was too sad and ashamed to run to Grandpa and Grandma's. She ran to a place on the bank of the pond where she liked to sit alone and think. She sat and sobbed until she was very tired. I'll run away, thought Marjorie Elisabeth Mousie. *But where can I go? Wherever I run, my feel will go with me.*

Al last, cold and hungry, Marjorie Elisabeth Mousie stood up to leave. But the bank had become slippery and Marjorie Elisabeth Mousie slipped down the bank and onto the ice of the frozen pond.

She skidded along for quite awhile. At first it was scary but her big feet kept her from falling.

Each time Marjorie Elisabeth took a step on the ice, she slid off in another direction. It was fun!

Marjorie Elisabeth Mousie found she could turn to the left by leaning left; to the right by leaning right. Once when she almost fell, she swung her arms around and found that this made her spin. What a wonderful time she was having! She forgot about the dancing class. Marjorie Elisabeth Mousie spun and glided fast as the wind over the ice.

She also forgot about the time. It had gotten dark when she heard voices calling her name and someone carrying a lantern. "Marjorie Elisabeth Mousie!" It was Grandpa out here on the ice.

"Here I am," called Marjorie Elisabeth.

"Marjorie Elisabeth Mousie, that's dangerous. Come here at once. Do you want to fall through the ice and drown?"

"I'm not going to fall through, Grandpa. My feet are just right for the ice."

"Well, just the same, Marjorie Elisabeth Mousie, come back. Everyone worried when you didn't come home from school."

Marjorie Elisabeth Mousie glided over to Grandpa.

"Why look at you, Marjorie Elisabeth Mousie, how fast you can go!"

"It is such fun, Grandpa! It is like dancing on ice."

"When leaves blow across the pond like that we say they are skating across the ice," said Grandpa. "That's what you are doing, Marjorie Elisabeth Mousie. You're skating! Now child, let's get you home and warm."

When Mother and Father Mousie heard what Marjorie Elisabeth Mousie had been doing, they were shocked and upset. "That's dangerous, Marjorie Elisabeth Mousie," said Father, "and you'll catch your death of cold out there on that ice. Marjorie Elisabeth, promise me now that you will not do that again."

"But skating is such fun," said Marjorie Elisabeth.

"Fun," Father replied, "it won't be fun when you fall through the ice. Now stay away from the pond, and that's that."

Poor Marjorie Elisabeth. Skating was so wonderful. It was special, too. She had never seen anyone else do it. But Marjorie Elisabeth Mousie was a well-behaved mousie and she did as her parents told her.

One night the snow began falling. It was the worst snowstorm Marjorie Elisabeth had ever seen. Her father went outdoors time after time to clear the snow away from the door and bring food to the animals. The storm went on. The wind blew and whistled around the house so hard and fast that one could see only the swirling white snow out the window.

The next morning the snow stopped. But Father began to cough. By noon, he was coughing badly and was hot with fever. Mother Matilda Mouse fed Father hot soup and piled blankets high over him but nothing helped.

"He needs Dr. Hooten," sighed Mother, "but how can we get him?"

Marjorie Elisabeth could see that Mother was very worried. She looked out the window and saw that though the snow had stopped falling, huge banks of the cold wet stuff lay everywhere. The roads were covered with high drifts of snow.

Then Marjorie Elisabeth noticed that the wind had blown the river clear of snow. She could see the ice sparkling in the sun. An idea formed in Marjorie Elisabeth's mind.

"Mother, I can get Dr. Hooten."

"How can you get the doctor, child? No one can get through this snow."

"Doesn't Dr. Hooten live on the river bank?"

"Yes," said Mother, "but a long way down the river."

"I will skate there, Mama. I can skate as fast as the wind that blew the snow last night."

"Oh, Marjorie Elisabeth, I don't know" said Mother but Father's cough was worse each hour.

Marjorie Elisabeth dressed warmly. "I've got to go, Mom, and get help for Father."

"Be careful, Marjorie Elisabeth."

"Please don't worry, Mom."

Marjorie Elisabeth walked slowly over the drifts toward the river, careful not

to sink in. Finally she was at the river's edge and stepped onto the ice.
"Now, here I go," said Marjorie Elisabeth. Glide, glide. Marjorie Elisabeth was whizzing down the ice faster and faster. Sooner than she could believe, Marjorie Elisabeth saw Dr. Hooten's home on the river bank.

Imagine how surprised Dr. Hooten was to see Marjorie Elisabeth.

"Come quickly, Dr. Hooten. My father is sick."

"But how can I get there, Marjorie Elisabeth? How did you get here?" asked old Dr. Hooten.

"I skated across the ice."

"Across the ice!" exclaimed Dr. Hooten. "Well, dear me, that is something new indeed. But I can't skate, Marjorie Elisabeth, and I really think I am too old to learn!"

"Please get your bag and coat, Dr. Hooten. I'll think of something," said Marjorie Elisabeth.

"Now let's see," said Marjorie Elisabeth, "what has big feet like me in this house? I know!" She looked at Dr. Hooten's rocking chair. "That's it!"

Dr. Hooten helped Marjorie Elisabeth carry the chair to the ice. He sat down, looking very worried.

"Don't worry, Dr. Hooten. This will work."

Dr. Hooten put a blanket across his knees, his bag on his lap and held on.

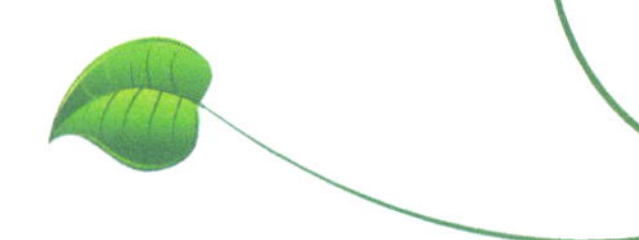

"Here we go," said Marjorie Elisabeth. Marjorie Elisabeth stood at the back of the rocking chair, took a hold of the side spokes and slowly, slowly pushed the doctor in the chair. It moved faster and faster.

Marjorie Elisabeth was so tired, and her feet were so cold. After a long while Marjorie Elisabeth's house came into sight.

Mother ran out of the house. "You did it, Marjorie Elisabeth. You did it, my wonderful mousie!"

Father was soon feeling well. Marjorie Elisabeth was a heroine! The whole town heard of how she saved her father by skating down the river to old Dr. Hooten's house.

Now all of the children wanted to see Marjorie Elisabeth skate. Marjorie Elisabeth skated her very best. Everyone was amazed. They especially liked seeing Marjorie Elisabeth spin around and they clapped loudly.

Well, dear readers, needless to say, Marjorie Elisabeth never worried about having friends again. And as far as having great big feet, she felt she was the luckiest mouse in the world.

Character Lesson:

Overcoming

A B C D E F G H I J   O P
4 × 2 = 8
7 × 7 =
Ollie Phant
Erin and Emily Vannoy
Illustrated by: Emily Vannoy

Ollie Phant

Erin and Emily Vannoy

It was a sunny Saturday when little Ollie Phant heard his mom call, "Ollie, you have mail!" She almost sang as he ran downstairs to breakfast. Ollie sat down at the table ignoring his bowl of cereal as he ripped open the tightly sealed envelope.

Ollie squealed as he read the headline. "You're invited to Foxy Brown's Crazy Carnival Birthday Blowout!"

Immediately, Ollie thought about the colorful cotton candies, the perfectly salted peanuts and the fountains of fizzy sugary sodas he would soon enjoy. He couldn't wait!

That Monday all the children in Mrs. Hasty's 3rd grade class had ants in their pants. Not one student could sit still. Foxy Brown's party was today after school and no one paid attention to the math problems Mrs. Hasty scribbled on the blackboard. Even worse, the clock read 8:15 a.m. Ollie signed. *I'll never make it all day,* he thought.

Quickly, Ollie threw a note to Ted Turtles. They had been buddies since last year in Mrs. Reeks' class. Her room had smelled of cigarettes and mothballs. According to Sarah

Snake, Mrs. Reeks had finally retired after 80 years. Ollie figured if he and Ted could get through Mrs. Reeks class last year, then one day in Mrs. Hasty's class should be a piece of cake.

The note bounced off Ted's shell. Luckily, Harriet Hare saw it and swept it up. But Mrs. Hasty had already noticed.

The note read: "I can't wait for tonight. Mrs. Hasty's class is so boring. What did you get Foxy for her birthday? —Ollie."

While Ted was reading, Mrs. Hasty said, "Patience, Ollie. You can speak to Ted at lunch. Do not let me see you not paying attention again."

Afterward, Mrs. Hasty was at the board writing her usual "phrase of the day." She must have heard about Foxy's party because her phrase was, "Good things come to those who wait." You could almost hear the students rolling their eyes as Mrs. Hasty talked about the importance of being patient. "Who cares?" Ollie thought. *They have doctors for patients.*

It seemed like a lifetime before the lunch bell rang. "Single file," yelled Mrs. Hasty. The lunchroom smelled of fish sticks and banana peels. Ollie could not even think of food. Standing in line, everyone was talking about the party. Fiona Fisher was yapping to the friend beside her about the gift she had gotten Foxy and Bill Bird was flapping his wings trying to explain the Ferris wheel to Larry Lions. It seemed no one had school on their mind.

After lunch and a short recess the class marched back into the classroom. No one was settling down and everyone was extra wild. Mrs. Hasty was not having it! "If you wild animals cannot sit still I will call Foxy's mother and

have her cancel the party!" Immediately the class was silent. Ollie looked at the clock and it was 1:30. "Two more hours," he winced.

Mrs. Hasty was instructing the class on a new assignment as Ollie's mind began to wander again. Bright blinking lights, crazy colored clowns, green gooey candied apples and flaky funnel cakes...

"Ollie? Do you know the answer?" asked Mrs. Hasty. She had noticed he wasn't paying attention.

"Peanuts!" Ollie exclaimed in a hurry. Ollie's head dropped as the class began to laugh.

"I have already asked you once to pay attention, Ollie. Now you will have to stay after school and unfortunately, you will be late to the party."

Warm tears filled Ollie's eyes. "The party; I'm going to be late!" he whimpered. The class continued with the lesson. Ollie slumped down in his chair. He was sorry.

A note from Ted Turtles went "smack" into Ollie's eye, jolting him backward. He knew if Mrs. Hasty caught him again he would be even later to the party, so he just waited.

All of a sudden, Ollie realized he had learned a valuable lesson. "That's it!" he proclaimed to himself. Mrs. Hasty was right. Good things do come to those who wait.

Ollie began to wipe the tears from his eyes and to himself he quietly vowed to always be patient.

Character Lesson:

Patience

18

Quacker of Avalon

Corinne Koonz-Pushman

Illustrated by: Jim O'Connell

Quacker of Avalon

Corinne Koonz-Pushman

In the spring of 2005, Quacker arrived at Avalon. He was placed in the lake behind our home. Quacker would paddle back n' forth, quacking all the while. That is how he got his name. Quacker would quack, quack, quack, and quack all day long. "Where am I? Why am I here? Where are my friends from the farm?"

One day as Quacker paddled around the lake he noticed something in the water. Was it a duck? It was big, though not as big as Quacker. It was not the same color as Quacker. What was trailing behind it?

As Quacker got closer, he noticed that they looked like him. They quacked like him. Quacker quacked, "Hello. How are you?"

They ignored him.

This time he quacked louder. "Who are you?"

The larger duck glared at him and said, "We are Mallard ducks. I am Mama Mallard and these are my Mallard ducklings, all nine of them. And who are you? You are so big with an orange bill and white feathers. Where did you come from?"

Mama Mallard sure can quack, Quacker thought. Then he said, "Well, nice meeting you."

"It is now feeding time," quacked Mother Mallard. "We must go."

Hmmmm. They weren't very friendly, Quacker thought as they started to swim away. *I do hope I will find a friend to quack with.*

When Quacker ran into the Mallard family again later, Mama Mallard made sure she stayed between the ducklings and Quacker, protecting them as all good Mamas do. "What do you want?" she asked.

"Oh, I thought we could be friends," said Quacker.

Mama Mallard glared thoughtfully at Quacker then answered, "I am much too busy to make friends. I must watch my ducklings very carefully to make sure they are doing their tasks correctly."

Quacker gave her a big smile and replied, "I can do that. I can help the ducklings do their tasks. I would make a very good duckling sitter."

Mama Mallard raised her eyebrows and laughed out loud. "Huh, I don't think so." She turned her back on Quacker and said to her ducklings, "Come, let's be on our way."

Quacker sat there looking very sad and forlorn. Gosh, I cannot make any friends here at all, he thought. I wish I was back at the farm. Quacker thought how much fun he had when he was back there. All the animals on the farm were so friendly and they all got along. Back n' forth, back n' forth, Quacker paddled away calling, "Quack, Quack, Quack, will someone be my friend?"

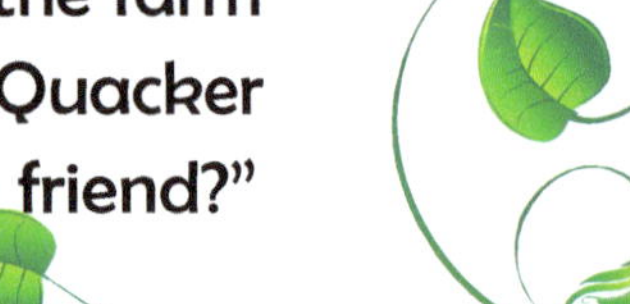

Days passed, even weeks. And Quacker swam back n' forth, back n' forth. "Quack, Quack, Quack." He would run into the Mallard family. When he tried to join them, Mama Mallard would put her head down and go after him, quacking the loudest quack. "I told you we are much too busy to be friends with you."

Quacker flapped his wings and replied, "Okay, okay, please do not pull my feathers. I am leaving."

Quacker has been at Avalon for several months. He noticed many houses with yards all around the lake. Quite a few humans would come out and work in their yards or have a barbeque. Quacker noticed one lady in particular. Whenever Quacker would go quacking by, she would quack back at him. One day the lady was standing at the edge of the lake. Every time Quacker quacked, so did the lady.

She would say, "Quack, Quack. Hi Quacker!"

Quacker thought, *how did she know my name?* The lady looked like a grandmother. *I think I will name her Grandma,* Quaker said to himself.

Grandma threw some bread into the water. Quacker paddled over and tried it. "Quack, Quack. That tastes so good. I will have to come back for more."

"See you again, Quacker," Grandma said and went into her house.

Quacker made daily trips across the lake and stopped at Grandma's house. Grandma would call, "Quack, Quack, Quack. Come and rest for awhile."

Grandma coaxed Quacker to come onto her patio. She would feed him bread or bird seed.

I have finally found a friend, thought Quacker. *I think I will rest here for awhile.* Quacker found a shady spot under a chair and fell fast asleep.

That was the beginning of a ritual. Every morning Quacker waddled onto the patio. He then tapped on the glass sliding door with his bill. "Quack, Quack. Wake up, Grandma. Quacker is here."

Grandma would come out to talk and feed Quacker. In the meantime, the Mallard ducklings were growing and swimming very well. They would play in the water and chase each other around the lake. As the ducklings became older, they became more curious about a white duck swimming back and forth, back and forth, quacking all day long. Some of the ducklings started following Quacker around. If they were naughty, Quacker would yank their back feathers and say, "Now you stop that, young Mallard."

One day, as Quacker made his daily trip to Grandma's house, the ducklings decided to follow. Curiosity even got the best of Mama Mallard. She too, followed. When they arrived at Grandma's house, Grandma came out and laughed and looked very surprised to see Quacker, nine ducklings and Mama Mallard.

"Well, well, what have we here?" asked Grandma. "I'd better get some more food to feed all of you. I did not expect all this company today."

After they were fed, Quacker decided to take a nap. The Mallard family did the same.

This, too, became a habit. Slowly, the Mallard family was accepting Quacker.

As summer passed by, the heat and humidity really worked overtime. During this hot spell, Grandma would be outside almost every day, watering her flowers and lawn when the Mallard family and Quacker would visit.

As they approached the patio, they could feel a spray. Grandma was playing with the ducklings. They would flap their wings and try to bite the water with their bills. This annoyed Quacker. He watched but didn't participate in the spraying water fun.

"Stop it!" he quacked. He then put his head down and chased the ducklings away. Quacker flapped his wings and quacked, "Quack, Quack. I am hungry."

Grandma looked at him, smiled and asked, "What is wrong?"

Quacker quacked scoldingly, "You are playing with the ducklings and you are not paying attention to me."

"Oh, I see," frowned Grandma. "Wait here." She walked back into her house. Minutes later, she returned with snacks and said, "You know, Quacker, the way to have a friend is to be one."

The Carolina summers are really hot, especially in August. The Mallard ducklings were becoming young ducks. They were learning to fly. Quacker was with them most of the time. He was teaching the young ducks how to dig up grubs with their bills.

Sometimes their bills would be black with mud from the lake. Their webbed feet would be black as well. Some of the Mallards moved on. It was time for them to fly away and seek their fortunes elsewhere, perhaps in another lake or pond. Quacker was now very patient with them. He taught them so much,

also how to take care of themselves. Quacker was becoming a real friend.

As September came, Quacker woke one morning and noticed it was very quiet and serene on the lake. Only two of the young ducks were left. They were a little slow in their flying abilities. They now stayed very close to Quacker. They followed him all around the lake, visiting other homes and digging for grubs. When Grandma came out to feed them they did not stay as they used to. They enjoyed the snacks then back into the lake they would go.

Sometimes the other Mallards would return and play with Quacker and the two young ducks. They would chase each other all over the lake. Best of all, they included Quacker in all their games.

Quacker was so happy! He had learned the true purpose of friendship. A friend accepts us as we are and shows us respect.

Now Quacker is keeper of the lake and is waiting for his friends to return in the spring. He still swims back and forth, back and forth, "Quack, Quack, Quack!"

Character Lesson:

Friendship.....is Life's dearest gift!

The only way to have a Friend is to be one.
Ralph Waldo Emerson

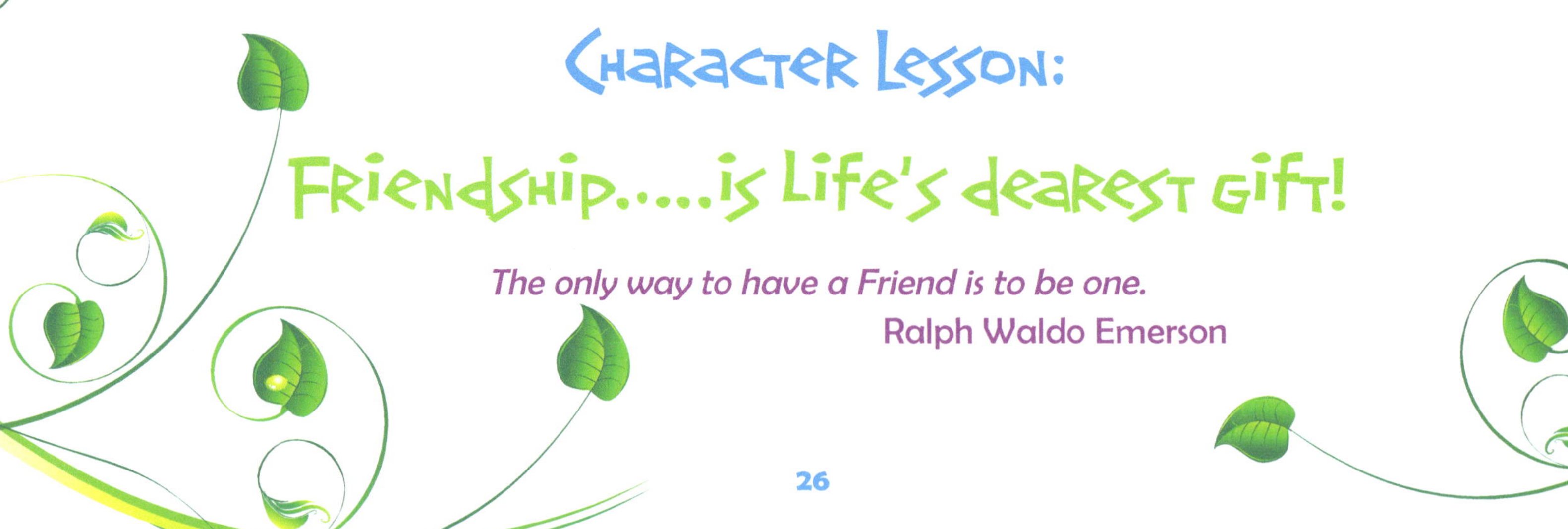

MSH
SwB
The Big Game
Vicki D. Westling
Illustrated by: Annette Asbill

The Big Game

Vicki D. Westling

The Sweetwater Bunnies were ready. It was Saturday at last and they were excited. It had been a long season and they had finally made it to the playoffs. Each game had been a hard one, but today's game was for the championship against their archrivals, the Moss Swamp Hares. Every rabbit on Clay Island was there. The bleachers were full and the fans were shouting and cheering before either team took to the field.

"We have to win this year," said Coach Haynes. "I want every bunny to play their best, and remember there is no glory in being the only one to make a goal if the team loses. Now, tighten your laces and let's kick grass!"

The Sweetwater Bunnies took to the field. Jimmy ran to the goalie cage and Bruce lined up in the forward position. As a forward, it was his job to score goals. Although any member of the team was allowed to score a goal, Bruce wanted to be the one to score the most. Bobby and Irene were assigned the position of guards. It was their job to defend against the other team and keep them from scoring a goal. And then there were the Hares at every opportunity. Other members of the team include Francis, Cody, Robert, Olivia, and Michael. Michael also played forward but on the opposite side of the field from Bruce.

Looking across the field to the other goal, Michael sighed. He was nervous. This was the first time his Daddy had been able to watch him play and he was not the best player on the team. He wanted to do well but he knew Bruce would be the one to score the most goals. Bruce was like that. He was almost a half year older than the others on the team and he was a lot bigger than Michael. Bruce was a good dribbler and he liked it when he could keep the ball all to himself taking it in for a goal without any assistance from his teammates. Michael looked at the goalie for the Moss Swamp Hares. He was huge. Then he looked over at the sidelines where his Mommy and Daddy were sitting. They raised their paws in a thumb up position and yelled, "Go Michael!" at the top of their lungs. Michael swallowed hard, turned and ran to his position on the field.

The referee blew the whistle and threw the ball in. His arm went around in a circle. The game began. The Bunnies and Hares were running and yelling, arms flying. The ball came at Michael so fast he almost didn't see it. He swung his right foot out and then his left. He moved down the field, dribbling the ball as fast as he could, and then whap! His face hit the ground. He saw the ball being stolen away by Bruce, his own teammate. He couldn't believe it.

Danny, one of the Hares, stole the ball from Bruce and all of the Bunnies moved toward Jimmy. Irene was trying to defend against the Hares and Bobby was running around to the other side of Danny. Olivia stopped and helped Michael up from the ground. "Come on, Michael. Let's get that ball back!"

Bruce put his foot out and Danny fell to the ground. The whistle blew. "Tripping!" yelled the referee. "Hares get the ball for a direct free kick and yellow penalty card goes to the Bunnies for tripping."

Coach Haynes called timeout. Bruce was benched and replaced by Charlie. Charlie was not a very good player and for the coach to remove Bruce had to be pretty serious. Michael swallowed hard. He thought his knees were shaking. This was a time he would have to step up. With Bruce out it would be his responsibility to keep the line moving and score some goals. "Okay, Bunnies, let's huddle," yelled Michael. "Now listen, we have to win this game. These guys are tough but we can do it. Let's set up. Everybody knows their position. We need to get the ball moving. Pass it off. It doesn't matter who scores just so we score more than the Hares."

The Bunnies were ready to play. They yelled and clapped their paws then ran onto the field. The crowd was quiet. The Hares were lined up and they looked mad.

The referee blew the whistle and the Hares threw in the ball. They moved it quickly down the field. Jimmy couldn't defend against their fast kick into the side of the net. The Bunnies were down 0-1 and the crowd roared. Bruce sat on the bench with his face in his hands. "I wouldn't have let that happen," he muttered.

"Ball in," yelled the referee. Irene stole the ball and dribbled it down the field. She passed it over to Cody who dribbled and then passed it to Olivia. The crowd was cheering loudly. Olivia was moving the ball down the field when Darren, one of the Hares, stole it. Darren dribbled and passed the ball to

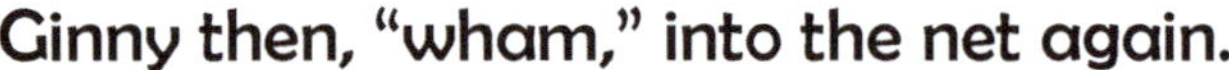

Ginny then, "wham," into the net again.

The Bunnies were down 0-2. Michael looked over at the bench. Bruce was begging the coach to let him back in.

"Time out," yelled Coach Haynes. "Everybody off the field," he called to the Bunnies. "Bruce is going back in. I'm sorry, Charlie."

The Bunnies ran back onto the field. The crowd booed when they saw Bruce run up to the Hares and shake his fist. "I'm back so you Hares better look out!" snarled Bruce.

The referee blew the whistle and yelled, "Ball in." The Bunnies ran after the ball and the Hares chased it down to the other end of the field. Bobby took possession and dribbled toward the sidelines then passed it over to Mary. Mary continued toward the goal posts then passed the ball to Johnny. Johnny was ready to make the kick into goal when Bruce ran up and stole the ball. The crowd booed! Bruce kicked the ball but the goalie for the Hares caught it and kicked it back to the middle of the field where the Hares were waiting for it. Bruce ran to the mid-line and grabbed the ball, elbowing Melissa, a Hare, in the face. She fell to the ground and he kicked the ball toward the sideline.

"Take Him Out!" the crowd called. "Red Card," yelled the Referee. Coach Haynes was not happy. "Time out!" he yelled.

When Bruce came to the bench this time, Coach Haynes was ready. "You know what, Bruce?" he began. "You are a good soccer player, you know the game and you can dribble the ball better than most of the Bunnies on the team. But you are all about you and Soccer is a team sport. Remove your

shin guards. You're out of the game."

Bruce sat on the bench and hung his head. He wanted to win this game so badly that he had forgotten about being a member of a team. After all, he was the oldest on the team and he felt it was his responsibility to win. But in reality, there were ten other players on the team and any one of them could score just as well as he could.

Bruce removed his shin guards, unlaced his cleats and then began cheering for all he was worth. "Go Bunnies! Come on, Michael, you can do it. Shoot the ball." Bruce walked up and down the sideline cheering his teammates on, directing them to where the ball was moving. "Go to your right, Irene. Look behind you, Johnny. You got it, Charlie. Dribble! The goal is yours!"

Charlie scored and the crowd went wild. The Hares got the ball on throw in but Mary stole it away. She dribbled down the field and passed the ball off to Robert. Robert took the ball down and passed it to Michael. "They Scored!" yelled Bruce.

The Bunnies had tied up the game, 2-2, and there were only three minutes left. The onlookers were on their feet. Again it was the Hares that got the ball on the throw in. Their forward, Bernice, dribbled it in front of the net and took one long swing of her hind foot and, "whap," another goal! The Bunnies were up 3-2.

"Time out," yelled coach Haynes. The Bunnies came off the field and huddled around the coach. "Listen, you all have played a wonderful game. Everyone has done their best. If we don't win this it is not because we haven't tried. Now, go back out there and have fun," said the coach. All of the Bunnies

jumped and cheered as they ran back onto the field.

Michael called to the other Bunnies. "We need to win. Let's do it for Coach Haynes!"

The Hares threw the ball in. Phillip got it and dribbled toward the goal where Jimmy was waiting. Phillip stood still and then kicked the ball. Jimmy caught it and threw it back to the center of the field where Cody was waiting. Cody passed the ball to Michael who was lined up at the side of the net. Michael kicked the ball. "Goal!" yelled the Referee. The Bunnies had tied up the game just as the whistle blew signaling the end of the game in regulation.

It was tense on the sidelines and the crowd was standing. The Bunnies had tied the score and now the game would go into overtime. The referee explained the rules and once again the tired Rabbits on both sides trotted onto the field. Each lined up in their position and the goalies wiped the sweat from their brows.

The referee blew the whistle. The ball was thrown in and once again the mad rush toward the goal began. First, the ball moved by the Hares toward Jimmy and then the Bunnies took it toward the Hare's goalie, Brad; and then back again. Bunnies and Hares were falling, sliding and missing the ball with their kicks. They were tired. Michael knew he had to do something.

"Bunnies, take a breath, and look around you. Get to the ball and keep it moving toward Brad," yelled Michael.

Olivia stole the ball and stood still with it between her feet before passing it off to Francis. Francis dribbled the best she could then she gave the ball over to Robert who then sent it across field to Johnny. Johnny took it up the sideline and then passed it to Michael who had lined up in front of the net. Michael knew he didn't have a chance to shoot the ball from where he was because there was a line of Hares waiting for him to kick the ball toward Brad. He looked around, and there was Mary standing at the corner of the net. He dribbled, faked toward Brad and then kicked the ball to Mary. "Mary!" he shouted. Mary saw the ball coming toward her. She was ready. She side-kicked the ball into the net. The crowd went wild! The whistle blew. The Bunnies had won just as time ran out.

As the Bunnies celebrated, they cheered and lifted Michael up on their shoulders, carrying him off the field. He had saved the game by sharing the glory of winning with his team.

"Great Job!" Coach Haynes shouted as the Bunnies surrounded him and cheered their win. Then all of the Bunnies lined up and went back on the field to shake paws with the Hares.

Bruce was too ashamed to share in the celebration. He hung his head and continued to sit on the bench when Michael came up to him.

"Don't look so sad, Bruce. Everyone knows you are a great player. We understand that you were just excited," said Michael.

"You know what, Michael?" Bruce began. "You are a good soccer player. I learned something today. I learned that soccer is a team sport and if we are to win, we have to play as a team. I didn't do that and I am sorry."

Coach Haynes walked up to the two players. "Soccer is like any other game;

it takes teamwork. But remember once the competition is over we can still be friends," said Coach Haynes. "We have ice cream and drink boxes courtesy of Michael's Daddy and Mommy. What do you say we invite the Hares to join us?"

"Come on, Bruce," said Michael. "Let's go celebrate our win."
Bruce, Michael and all of the other Bunnies ran over to the sideline where the Hares were gathered. "Come on, Hares, let's have ice cream," yelled Michael.

Character Lesson:

Teamwork- one person is not a team; it takes everyone to work together as a team, that's how we all win.

Rufus the Rooster Meets Larry the Fox
Vicki Westling
Illustrated by: Annette Asbill

Rufus the Rooster Meets Larry the Fox
Vicki Westling

Rufus struggled to awaken. He could barely see the sun beginning to climb over the horizon and he knew that it was time for him to do his job. He looked around the barnyard. The chickens were all snuggled in their nests sound asleep with their heads tucked beneath their wings. The baby piglets and their mommy were curled up against the bail of hay Farmer John had placed in their pen. The cows were resting peacefully beneath the apple trees in the pasture. Even the horses were snoring in their stalls in the barn.

Rufus looked over at the big white farmhouse. Not a light was on. Old Blue, the floppy-eared hound dog, was asleep in his doghouse with only his nose sticking out. "It isn't fair," thought Rufus. "I have to get up every day. I never get to sleep in." He stomped his foot and tucked his head back under his wing. "Well, today all that ends."

But Rufus was not the only one awake. Larry, the sly red fox, was watching Rufus. Larry had been keeping his eye on the henhouse for some time. He could almost taste the juicy fat chickens. The only thing between him and a feast fit for a king was Rufus, the big red rooster who guarded the henhouse.

Larry climbed the fence and quietly slipped up to the perch where Rufus slept. Before Rufus knew what hit him, Larry threw a burlap feed sack over Rufus' head. Rufus squawked and squirmed but it was not use. Everyone was still sleeping soundly so there was no one to come to his rescue.

Larry ran with the sack as fast he could. He jumped back over the fence and hurried off into the woods. Soon he stopped and put the sack on the ground next to the little stream. Then with all of his might he pushed a big rock on one end of the sack so Rufus couldn't get out. Licking his lips, Larry quietly slipped back through the woods and into the barnyard. It was getting light and Larry knew he would have to hurry if he was to get the chickens out of their nests before Mitchell came out to feed them and collect the eggs for breakfast. But Mitchell was fast asleep.

Slipping into the henhouse, Larry could barely keep quiet. He was so excited. He grabbed the first hen, Isabella, and tossed her into a sack, then on to Martha, Betty, Millie and Veronica. He quickly tied the end of the sack and tossed it against the door. Then he started down the other aisle. He startled Sally and she began to squawk. But he got her into the sack and put Linda in on top of her. Not wanting to leave anyone in the henhouse, Larry took one last look around. There was Natalie hiding beneath a stool. He put her in with Sally and Linda and then tied the top of the sack.

Pulling both sacks along the ground, he dragged the chickens through the door of the henhouse and out the gate. The sacks were heavy and he struggled as he dragged them into the woods and to the stream where he had left Rufus. He placed rocks on the end of each sack so the chickens couldn't escape and then gathering sticks and twigs so he could build a fire.

The hens were scared. "Where are we?" squawked Natalie.

"I think we are in the woods somewhere," replied Linda.

"Do you think the others are here, too?" asked Sally.

"We're here, too," said Millie from the other sack.

"Who is in there with you?" asked Natalie.

"Isabella, Martha, Betty and Veronica," answered Millie.

"Who nabbed us?" asked Isabella, "and why?"

Rufus answered, "I know who—and why."

"Rufus!" all the hens squawked at the same time.

"Rufus," said Linda, "you have to help us."

"I can't help you," said Rufus sorrowfully. "I am the reason you are in this mess. It is because of me that Larry was able to sneak in and nab all of you. It was Larry who took you and he plans to have himself a fine feast."

"Well, we can't just stay in these sacks and wait for Larry to come back and eat us," said Isabella. "We have to do something."

"Maybe Mitchell will wake up and come save us," said Rufus. "He is our only hope. Let's begin making as much noise as we can. Maybe he will hear us." All the chickens started cackling and squawking as loudly as they could, and Rufus began to cock-a-doodle-doo with all the energy he could muster.

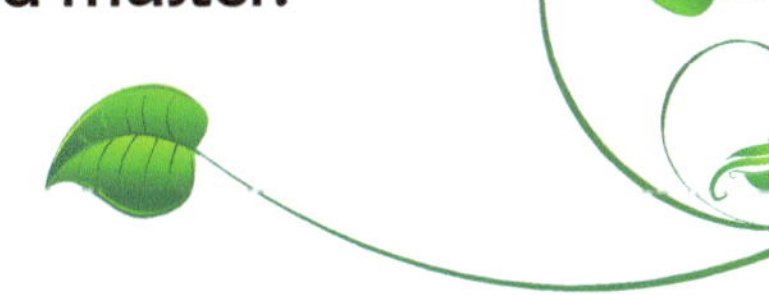

They were making a mighty noise and the other animals in the woods heard them and knew there was something going on. They, too, began to make their morning sounds.

Mitchell was only seven years old but he was very responsible. It was his job to feed Rufus and the chickens every morning and then gather the eggs from their nests. But today it wasn't Rufus's cock-a-doodle-doo that woke him; it was the sun shining in through the window and warming his face. He rubbed his eyes and smiled. Then he looked at the clock. 7:00 A.M.

Mitchell jumped out of bed and ran outside. It was very quiet. He ran into the barnyard. There were no chickens squawking. The cows weren't mooing. The pigs weren't oinking. The entire barnyard was silent. All of the animals were still sleeping in their pens and stalls, all except the chickens and Rufus. They were gone.

The door to the chicken coop stood open and the gate from the chicken yard was open, too. Mitchell went into the chicken yard and looked around. No chickens and no Rufus!

He went into the barn and let Ben the horse out of his stall. He gave him some fresh hay. But he didn't see Rufus.

He climbed up the ladder into the hayloft, but no Rufus.

He went down to the cow pasture. Still no Rufus.

He ran to the pigpen but there was still no sign of Rufus. Where could he be?

Mitchell began to search for Rufus. There must be a clue, he thought. He knew Rufus wouldn't just leave on his own. Rufus had always been very dependable. Mitchell went to the chicken yard and searched every inch of it. He went to the roost where Rufus usually sat. There he saw a feather.

Mitchell bent down and picked up the feather. It looked like it came from Rufus' wing. He walked toward the fence. There was another feather. It looked like it came from Rufus' tail.

Mitchell was scared. He looked closer and saw four paw prints in the soft earth. They went back and forth across the yard to the hen house and out the gate. "A fox!" he yelled.

"Mommy, Daddy, come quick. I think Rufus has been rooster-napped by a fox!" But Mommy and daddy were still asleep and they didn't hear him.

"I must find Rufus," Mitchell said out loud. He stood very still and listened. He held the two feathers up to the wind and listened. Then he heard what sounded like a rooster cock-a-doodle-dooing and chickens cackling and squawking. He followed the sounds.

Creeping through the woods, Mitchell was scared. He tried to be quiet as he tiptoed on the moist ground. He was careful not to step on fallen twigs as he walked. He didn't want to make any noise. He knew Larry was probably somewhere nearby and he wanted to make sure he got to the chickens first.

But Larry saw Mitchell. He had heard the commotion the chickens and Rufus were making and he, too, had decided to go check things out. He watched Mitchell slipping around trees and stepping over small bushes. But Larry was sly. He walked along the trees taking cover when he needed to in order to keep Mitchell from seeing him.

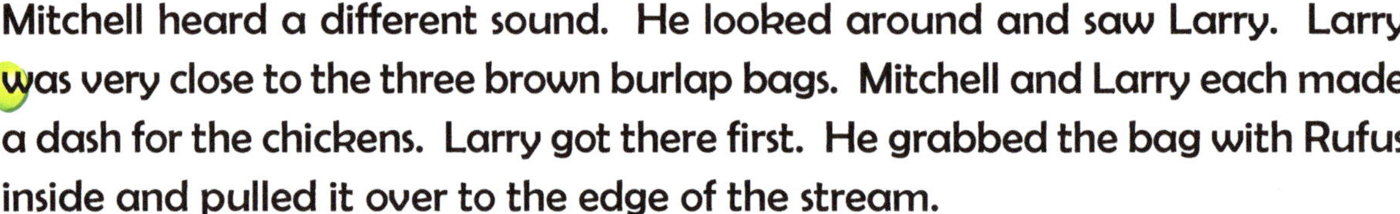

Mitchell heard a different sound. He looked around and saw Larry. Larry was very close to the three brown burlap bags. Mitchell and Larry each made a dash for the chickens. Larry got there first. He grabbed the bag with Rufus inside and pulled it over to the edge of the stream.

"Let him go, Larry," shouted Mitchell.

"No, Mitchell. You leave or I will throw Rufus over the cliff and into the water," Larry growled back.

Mitchell tried to pull the other two bags free of the rocks holding them down without Larry seeing him. "Okay, Larry, I will leave, but you need to put Rufus down. We need him."

Mitchell got the rocks off one of the bags. He motioned to the chickens inside and Linda, Natalie and Sally quietly slipped out and hid behind a tree.

Mitchell began working on the second bag. "Larry, maybe we can talk about this. You don't want to eat Rufus," Mitchell said in his calmest voice, "and you surely don't want to throw him over that cliff."

"You are right, Mitchell, I don't want to eat him or throw him over the cliff. I want those tasty, plump, juicy hens. That's what a fox does. Now move away from those bags and I will let you have Rufus."

The second bag was open. Mitchell motioned for the hens to walk out quietly and stay low to the ground so Larry couldn't see them. Once Millie, Isabella, Martha, Betty and Veronica were safely out of the sack and behind the tree with the others, Mitchell began to walk toward Larry.

Larry looked around him. There was no place for him to run. The cliff was in front of him and there was a big tree behind him. Worse yet, there was no one to help him. He felt all alone. He didn't have any friends like Rufus and the chickens did. Mitchell had friends, and even the squirrels and other woodland animals had friends to play with and help them. But not Larry. He felt sad.

He was just hungry. Why did he always have to fight for his food? He wanted to belong but he just didn't know how. He didn't really want to hurt Rufus and although he thought the taste of the fat juicy hens would be delightful, he didn't really want to hurt them either. But what else could he do?

"Look, Mitchell," Larry began, "I have to eat, too. I need a place to live and I want to belong. Do you think I like being out here all alone?"

The animals in the woods were all watching. This was a showdown they had been waiting for. Larry had been the bully of the woods for a long time and they were happy to see him put in his place.

"Larry," Mitchell said, "if you will set Rufus free and stop bullying the other animals we can make a place for you at our farm. You will be given a house, food every day and you will have the job of patrolling the fence line to make sure all the animals are safe."

"Why would I want to work for my food, Mitchell?" asked Larry. "Besides, what kind of a job could I do?"
"Everyone at the farm has a job to do and sometimes that job isn't easy. There are temptations and days when we just don't want to get out of bed but we are responsible for doing our share of the work. If you let Rufus go you will have a job, too. You will be responsible." Mitchell continued walking

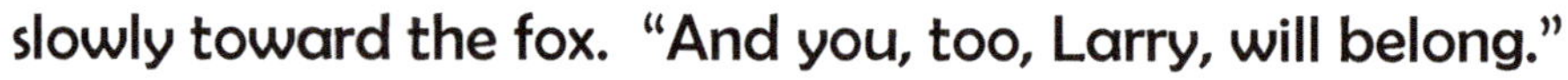

slowly toward the fox. "And you, too, Larry, will belong."

The animals in the woods began to chant, "Let Rufus Go. Be Responsible! Let Rufus Go. Be Responsible!"

The chickens joined in from behind the tree where they had been hiding. "Let Rufus Go. Be Responsible!"

Larry didn't know what to do. He didn't want to look weak but he knew Mitchell and the others were right. He set the bag down and opened the end. "Go ahead, Rufus. You are free."

Rufus walked over to the hens. They all hugged him.

Mitchell shook Larry's paw. The animals among the trees applauded and cheered. Then Rufus turned around toward Mitchell.

"Mitchell," said Rufus, "I am sorry. It is my fault this happened. I was tired this morning and I wanted to sleep in like everyone else. But now I realize everyone has a job to do even when we don't want to do it. That is what responsibility is all about. I won't disappoint you again." Rufus put out his wing toward Mitchell and the two shook, hand to wing.

As the animals in the woods cheered, Rufus, the hens, Larry and Mitchell all walked from the woods and back to the farm where Mommy and Daddy were waiting.

Rufus never neglected his responsibility again. Every morning, just as the sun began to peek over the horizon, he stood proudly and cock-a-doodle-dooed at the top of his lungs. The chickens laid their eggs and Larry patrolled the fence line to make sure everything and everyone was safe.

Character Lesson:

Responsibility, everyone has a job to do

that others depend upon.

The Special Gift
Pat Orrell
Illustrated by: Matthew Smiley

The Special Gift
Pat Orrell

"Mama, Mama, you'll never guess what. We got kittens!" yelled six-year-old Lisa. "We got kittens in my closet and Miss Foggy is taking care of them."

"Well, Lisa," laughed Mother, "our gray cat, Miss Foggy, is the kittens' mommy."

"Look, Mama, Miss Foggy likes her kittens. She is licking them all over. I guess she's giving them a bath. Miss Foggy almost looks like she smiling. The kittens are climbing all over her and she just purrs and purrs. She's a happy cat mother."

"I really think you're right about that, Lisa. But now let's leave Foggy and her kittens alone."

Every day when Lisa came home from school she ran upstairs to watch the kittens. Their eyes were open now and they climbed all over on wobbly kitten feet.

Lisa gave the four kittens names. The orange one was called Sunshine, the black one with a white spot on its nose was called Snowflake, the kitten with the black mark over its eye was called Pirate and the little one with mixed-up colors of white, black and orange was called Patches.

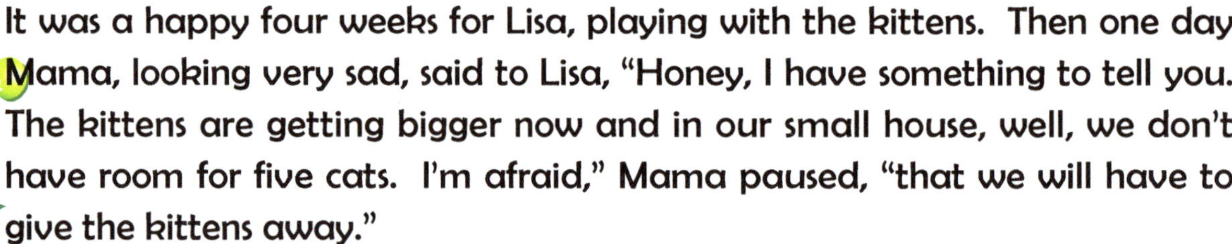

It was a happy four weeks for Lisa, playing with the kittens. Then one day Mama, looking very sad, said to Lisa, "Honey, I have something to tell you. The kittens are getting bigger now and in our small house, well, we don't have room for five cats. I'm afraid," Mama paused, "that we will have to give the kittens away."

"No, Mother. No," Lisa pleaded.

"Now, now, Lisa, I have found homes for them with people who love cats. We will still keep Miss Foggy and the kitten you call Patches. No one has chosen Patches because they don't think he is a cute cat.

"Oh," said Lisa, Patches is a beautiful cat and she's smart, too. She sits with me when I read and I really think she listens to me because she doesn't move."

Mother sighed. "So, for now, we'll have Miss Foggy and Patches. But we will also need to find a home for Patches or we'll have to take her to the shelter. Don't look so sad Lisa. The shelter finds homes for kittens, too."

"But," sobbed Lisa, "They will put Patches in a cage. What if no one wants Patches, Mother? What then?"

"Well, Lisa, let's just keep trying," said Mother.

"I will try and try," cried Lisa. "Patches will have a good home."

Lisa asked everyone in school "Wouldn't you like a kitten?"

The children said, "Yes!" but the parents said, "No, no, no!"
A very unhappy Lisa walked home from school. She waved to Mrs. Allen.

Mrs. Allen sat in her wheelchair on her porch enjoying the sun. Mrs. Allen lived alone except for a lady who came to help her sometimes because she couldn't do too much herself.

Mrs. Allen had arthritis, Lisa's mother told her. "It's a very painful disease in her bones," mother had said. Still Mrs. Allen waved at Lisa and smiled.

When Lisa walked into her home, Mother had fresh-baked sugar cookies waiting for her to eat.

As Lisa was eating a cookie she had an idea. She wrapped up four cookies in a napkin and got Patches from upstairs.

"Mother," called Lisa, "I'm going next door to Mrs. Allen's house." "Fine, Lisa," Mother called back.

Lisa carried the cookies and Patches to Mrs. Allen's porch.

"Well, Lisa, what do you have there?" asked Mrs. Allen.

"I brought you some sugar cookies, Mrs. Allen," responded Lisa.

"Oh, what a treat," said Mrs. Allen. "But what is that little bundle in your arms?"

"This is Patches, Mrs. Allen, the friendliest kitten in the World! Would you like to hold her?"

"Well, yes I would," smiled Mrs. Allen.

Patches sat down on Mrs. Allen's lap and began to purr.
"What a lovely kitten," said Mrs. Allen. "I think she likes me."

"She sure does, Mrs. Allen. She doesn't purr that fast for just anyone," said Lisa.

"Well, well, now," said Mrs. Allen. "This is very nice."

"Would you like to keep the kitten?" whispered Lisa. "She has a bowl and a litter pan. I can bring some food and I'll stop in every day to feed her for you. Would you like her, Mrs. Allen? Would you, please?"

"Well, yes," said Mrs. Allen. "Yes. This kitten is just what I needed, and if you will help me take care of her, I would like to keep her!"

"Oh, wonderful!" sighed Lisa. "I'll go get her stuff right now."

When Lisa got back to Mrs. Allen's porch she saw the kitten still sitting on Mrs. Allen's lap, still purring, and Mrs. Allen still smiling.

"What will you name your kitten?" asked Lisa.

"I am going to name this kitten Blessing because that is just what she is to me," said Mrs. Allen. "Thank you, Lisa."

"You're welcome, Mrs. Allen. I'll be back tomorrow."

As Lisa walked away Mrs. Allen said, "And you are a blessing, too, Lisa. A real blessing."

Character Lesson:

Compassion

About the Authors:

Patricia Orrell:

Patricia Glenn Orrell was born in New Haven, Connecticut. She attended Southern Connecticut University earning a B.S. degree in Primary Education with a major in Art and also holds a Master's degree in Art from Columbia University. Patricia enjoys traveling with her husband throughout Europe and the Bahamas. She now lives in Myrtle Beach, South Carolina, the perfect place to indulge in all her interests, especially writing, art and travel.

Corinne Koonz-Pushman:

Corinne-Koonz Pushman was born and raised in New York. She has always enjoyed writing since childhood. Corinne retired from the Wallkill school system. Her main focus in life is spending time with husband, Albert, her four sons and daughter in-laws and her five grandchildren.

Erin and Emily Vannoy:

Erin Vannoy is a recent graduate from Coastal Carolina University with a BA in psychology. She is working with at risk youths and plans on continuing her education in the future. Erin is very excited and proud of Adventure Tails, her first publication. Emily is working on her BA at Coastal Carolina University and works at a local restaurant. Emily

has been published in a local High School creative-writing book and is looking forward to future projects. Erin and Emily Vannoy currently live together in Myrtle Beach, SC where they continue to read and write.

Vicki Westling:

Mrs. Westling holds a degree in business management and professional instructor certificates in Florida and New York. She has taught reading, English and composition at the elementary, high school and college levels. She and her husband Richard reside in Dunkirk, New York, with their dog, Sam. She is the author of a novel, Thunder of Silence and a Sam and Friends children's book series. Mrs. Westling has been published in professional magazines, local newspapers and newsletters. Her passion is writing and spending time with her husband, their dog, and two very special sisters, Jan and Annette, and her son Glenn.

The Illustrators:

Annette Asbill

Jim O'Connell

Matthew Smiley

Emily Vannoy

www.ingramcontent.com/pod-product-compliance
Lightning Source LLC
Chambersburg PA
CBHW041356010726
47507CB00002B/170